/ 4.99   C. 1   3/0

**DATE DUE**

PowerKids Readers:
# Nature Books™

# Sand

Kristin Ward

The Rosen Publishing Group's
PowerKids Press™
New York

For Thomas and Mak, with love

Published in 2000 by The Rosen Publishing Group, Inc.
29 East 21st Street, New York, NY 10010

Copyright © 2000 by The Rosen Publishing Group, Inc.

First Edition

Book design: Michael de Guzman

Photo Credits: p. 1 by Donna M. Scholl; p. 5 CORBIS/Dewitt Jones; p. 7 © Don Hebert/FPG International; p. 9 © Bob Firth/FPG International; p. 11 © Judy Curuvitz/International Stock; p. 13 © Frank Cezus/FPG International; p. 15 © Cotter/International Stock; p. 17 © Digital Vision; p. 19 © Andre Hote/International Stock; p. 21 © Ron Chapple/FPG International.


Ward, Kristin.
    Sand / by Kristin Ward.
    p.  cm. — (Nature books)
Includes index.
Summary: Describes what sand is and where it is commonly found.
ISBN  0-8239-5530-3
1. Sand Juvenile literature. [1. Sand.] I. Title. II. Series: Nature books (New York, N.Y.)
QE471.2.W37 1999
553.6'22—dc21                                    98-49732
                                                      CIP
                                                       AC


Manufactured in the United States of America

# Contents

Sand is tiny pieces of rock.

There is a lot of sand at the beach.
Some beaches are near oceans.

Some beaches are near lakes.

9

You can find seashells in the sand.

11

Some crabs live in the sand near the ocean. These sand crabs dig holes to hide in.

13

People dig in the sand, too. They like to make sand castles.

Beaches are not the only places that have sand. Deserts have sand, too.

The biggest desert in the world is the Sahara desert in Africa.

19

Many parks have sandboxes. Some kids like to play in the sand.

# Words to Know

BEACH

LAKE

OCEAN

SAND

SAND
CASTLE

SAND
CRAB

SANDBOX

SEASHELLS

Here are more books to read about sand:

*At the Beach*
by Anne F. Rockwell, illustrations by Harlon Rockwell

*Beachy Keen:  A Fun and Educational Look at Everything About the Beach for Kids*
By Carole Marsh
Gallopade Publishing Group

To learn more about sand, check out this Web site:
http://www.netaxs.com/~sparky/sand_gallery.html

# Index

Word Count: 98

## Note to Librarians, Teachers, and Parents

PowerKids Readers (Nature Books) are specially designed to help emergent and beginning readers build their skills in reading for information. Simple vocabulary and concepts are paired with photographs of real kids in real-life situations or stunning, detailed images from the natural world around them. Readers will respond to written language by linking meaning with their own everyday experiences and observations. Sentences are short and simple, employing a basic vocabulary of sight words, as well as new words that describe objects or processes that take place in the natural world. Large type, clean design, and photographs corresponding directly to the text all help children to decipher meaning. Features such as a contents page, picture glossary, and index help children get the most out of PowerKids Readers. They also introduce children to the basic elements of a book, which they will encounter in their future reading experiences. Lists of related books and Web sites encourage kids to explore other sources and to continue the process of learning.

24